Josephine A. Smith

Being Cool, Going To School

Pictures by
May Dowley

Edited by
Natalie Wilkins

JOSEPHINE A. SMITH

BEING COOL, GOING TO SCHOOL

pictures by

MAY DOWLEY

edited by

NATALIE WILKINS

Published by Hickle Pickle Publishing 1994

4450 Allison Dr.
Michigan Center, MI 49254

ISBN: 1-881958-02-7

Library of Congress Catalogue Card Number: 92-074244

This book is dedicated to the 1953 and 1954 graduating class of Jackson High School, Jackson, Michigan.

I remember the good times we shared.

Acknowledgements:
A special thanks to Pickle Packers International
for their help and information.

The cool breeze felt good on Hickle's face as he rolled over in his warm bed. He grabbed his blanket and started to fall back to sleep when he heard a knock at the door. "Time to get up, Hickle. Today's the day you go to school." Hickle opened his eyes, looking around his room. He remembered the day he ran away from the garden, and the day he was found and entered in the fair. He remembered how he felt when he won first prize and how excited he was to become a dill pickle. Now, for some strange reason, he was a real person. He was green, but otherwise, just like other children. He was having so much fun as a little boy that he didn't want to stop, but there are things all kids have to do, and going to school is one of them. Without school, you can't read or write or get an important job. He found out about that already! So he agreed to go to school so he could be important someday...when he had grown up. Hickle snuggled down in his bed, wondering why it always feels better when it's time to get up than it does when you go to bed. Oh well, he thought, there's more to life than sleeping, and today was the first day of his new life. He looked over at the chair where Sarah laid his clothes so nice and neat. He didn't want to put on clothes; they were hot and felt funny. Normally, all he wore was a bow tie and top hat. Those days were gone, he thought sadly. He looked at his hat and bow tie which sat on the bed post, and smiled. He got up and went into the bathroom to take a bath and get clean for school. Afterward, he dried off, put on his blue jeans, shirt, and tennis shoes and looked in the mirror, thinking, "Boy, I sure look different." He sadly looked back at his room as he left.

"I'm all ready!" he said to Sarah who was standing by the stove cooking something which smelled good. She placed it on the plate in front of Hickle.

"Are you scared?" she asked, concerned.

"A little bit. But after all I've been through, I think I can manage." She patted him on the head and smiled. It had been enjoyable with Hickle here. Although it was late August when she found him at the pickle factory, the last couple of weeks were quite an experience. Teaching him right from wrong and helping him get used to responsibilities was a full-time job. He had such a way of expressing himself that she was sure he would be a joy to his teacher. She looked at the clock. It was time. "Well Hickle, you'd better wash your hands and get your jacket. It's time to leave for school." Hickle's stomach felt funny, like the jello he had for supper.

"I don't feel so good, Sarah." She smiled, for she knew he had butterflies, and told him so. "You've got butterflies in your stomach," she said. He looked at her. "How'd they get in there?" he said, covering his mouth.

"Oh, Hickle, that's just an expression. It means your stomach feels fluttery," said Sarah, laughing at Hickle's remarks. Hickle couldn't understand this crazy language. He picked up his pad, pencil, crayons and a box with his name on it. Sarah carried a small rug. Hickle felt like he was moving, seeing all his things leave for who knows where.

In the distance, he spotted the school. Sarah parked the car and walked him to his room. The other boys and girls were laughing and snickering. He couldn't figure out why until one boy said, "Why are you green? Are you from outer space or something?" The other children gathered around him and poked fun at him. Hickle's head dropped, as tears formed in the corners of his eyes. He wanted to be like them, but he wasn't...he was green.

During the next few weeks, he learned how to play, listen to the teacher read and take a nap on his rug. He still had no friends and felt very lonely. One day, a little boy came over to him.

"Hickle, I don't have any friends either. Will you be my friend?" he asked.

"Yes," Hickle said, and smiled at the young boy who he had made happy. Hickle and Jimmy played on the swings and monkey bars together. They had fun and laughed at each other's mistakes. The other children laughed at them and called them weird. Jimmy was also a different color, so Hickle and Jimmy had something in common.

Some days, they would just sit on the school steps and talk. Those were the happiest days for Hickle. He told Jimmy about running away from home and finding what he was looking for right in his own home, when he returned. Jimmy told him that he was born far, far away, across the big water. His mother was killed during a war and he was an orphan. Hickle thought maybe he was an orphan, too. He never had a mother or father. Jimmy and Hickle were good friends and were very much alike. Jimmy was adopted, and in a way, so was Hickle.

"I don't mind being adopted. At least, I have a mother and father now. Before, I didn't have anybody who cared. It's fun to have parents who love you and who

picked you out from a letter." Hickle said, "I was picked up off the floor." Jimmy fell over laughing.

"Oh, Hickle, you looked so funny when you said that." Hickle also laughed. It WAS funny after he thought about all the people sliding on the slippery floor when he fell out of the vat.

"Boys and girls," said the teacher. "Friday is Halloween. We will be having a party and you may dress up." Hickle looked at Jimmy who was all smiles.

"What's Halloween?" he asked the teacher amid snickers from the other children.

"He must have come from Mars," said one of the other boys.

"Children! Not all children have the opportunities you have. Some children come from lands where Halloween isn't celebrated, so be nice. Hickle, your homework will be to find out all about Halloween."

On the way home, he asked Sarah about Halloween.

"On Halloween, boys and girls dress up and go to parties. Then, at night, they go house to house and knock on the door, saying 'Trick or treat!' The person answering the door gives them candy and then they go to another house."

"Why?" asked Hickle.

"It goes back a long time. It's a tradition."

"What's a tradition?" Sarah smiled and shook her head.

"Let's go to the library and find out why we celebrate Halloween."

That night, Sarah and Hickle went to the library. Hickle looked up at the

beautiful building. He felt funny walking through the brass doors. The floors were made of large black and white squares and he tried not to step on the cracks. He remembered a game they played in school. "If you step on a crack, you break your mother's back." He didn't want anything to happen to Sarah ...ever.

They went into a large room, where she asked a boy behind a desk to help her. The boy found a book called Holidays and Sarah looked through it until she found Halloween.

"Hickle, listen," she said as she read out loud to him. "Halloween used to be celebrated in May and was called All Saints' Day, or All Hallows' Day. It was shifted to November by some person called Gregory III in the Eighth Century. November 1st, All Saints' Day was followed by All Souls' Day, November

2nd. Then, in England, they stopped All Souls' Day but kept on celebrating All Saints' Day. Why it was changed to October was not mentioned in the book."

"Trick or treat, an American custom, is a Halloween treat for little children. It is related to a practice of giving cakes to the poor at summer's end, kind of like paying for a good harvest. Another concept was English Plough (Plow) Day. Plowmen went about begging for gifts, and if they did not receive anything, threatened damage to the grounds with their plows."

The next day was Halloween. Hickle had to dress up and he didn't want to.

"Sarah, I don't want to put that on. Why can't I be something else?" he asked as he pouted in the corner. She put the costume back in the box. He went upstairs and took his bow tie and hat off the bed post and ran downstairs.

"Can I just put these on?"

"No, you have to wear clothes." Sarah thought and thought and finally came up with an idea. "How would you like to dress as a ghost?"

"Can I wear my hat and tie?"

"Yes, you can wear your hat, but let's leave the tie home." She went upstairs and cut up an old sheet. Placing it over Hickle's head, she marked where the eyes and mouth are and took it off to cut out the circles. Then she put it back on. Hickle put on his hat and looked in the mirror. Turning around, he yelled, "BOO!"

"Oh Hickle, you scared me!" said Sarah, pretending.

"I'm sorry." He put his arm around her neck and kissed her on the cheek and she laughed.

"Were you really scared?"

"Yes, I was."

"Good, now no plowman will get me, 'cause I'll scare him." Sarah wished she had never told him about that.

All the way to school, Hickle saw children walking with their costumes on. He felt better knowing he too was dressed up and they would have fun guessing who he was.

BOO!

In school, the children all lined up and walked around to the different rooms.

Children laughed at Hickle because of his hat. They pulled on his sheet and he had to stop and arrange the cutouts again, so he could see. Finally the teacher put a pin through the hat and sheet so they would stay in place. It worked! Hickle had fun! Later that night, he went "trick or treating" with Sarah. He got bags full of candy and later they sat on the floor sorting out what he wanted and what she said he could have. He ate so much he was full. He ate popcorn balls, which were his favorite, and candy bars, peanut butter cups and kisses. Finally, holding onto his tummy, he went to bed.

The next day, the teacher had a project for the class.

"Class, soon it will be Thanksgiving, the celebration of the landing of the pilgrims at Plymouth Rock. It should make you feel good that your ancestors decided to live here in the United States. I would like you to find out where your family came from, and what you have to be thankful for. Ask your mom and dad to help you find your family roots." Hickle laughed to himself, because he knew where his roots were, over on Orange Street in some little back yard garden. He thought about other cucumbers, ones which were part of his family. Some made it to become pickles and others didn't. He wondered where his family came from. He wondered if he had a heritage.

When Sarah picked him up, she knew something was wrong.

"Want to talk about it?" she asked.

"No, probably won't do any good. You can't help me this time," he said, dropping his head and kicking his feet back and forth.

"Maybe I can. Why don't you tell me and see?"

"We have to trace our family roots in school. I don't have any roots. The kids were laughing at me, saying I should check on Mars and find out if my family lives there. Where is Mars, and did my family come from there?"

"No, Hickle, you didn't come from Mars, but we will find out where you did come from. We'll go back to the library." Hickle thought the library must have answers to all the questions in the whole world. He felt better knowing he would find out where he came from.

That night, they went back and looked through books on foods, books on cucumbers, books on making pickles, books on everything except where pickles originated. Hickle couldn't find anything telling him where they came from and when.

"You might have to go to a bigger library," a librarian told them.

"We will. We will go to the state library tomorrow." The next day, Sarah called the state library and talked to a librarian.

"Do you have any books on the origin of dill pickles?" she asked. The librarian punched "Dill Pickles" into the computer, which came up with How to make Dill Pickles, and books on other products using pickles. But most of the books were on the use of dill pickles and nothing on the origin. "However, if you would like to come up and look around, I'm sure we could find something to help you."

Sarah thought of the long drive and felt discouraged. She looked at the clock and left to pick up Hickle.

"Are we going to the state library?" he asked enthusiastically.

"No, I called there and they couldn't tell me anything. I'm afraid there's no way for us to find out where you came from. Hickle, you'll just have to forget about your family tree."

"But I can't. All the kids poke fun at me. They say I came from Mars and if I don't have a family tree, they'll believe I did. Please help me!" he cried.

Sarah looked at the little guy sitting all bent over crying. He looked so sad! She knew right then and there she would help him find his heritage.

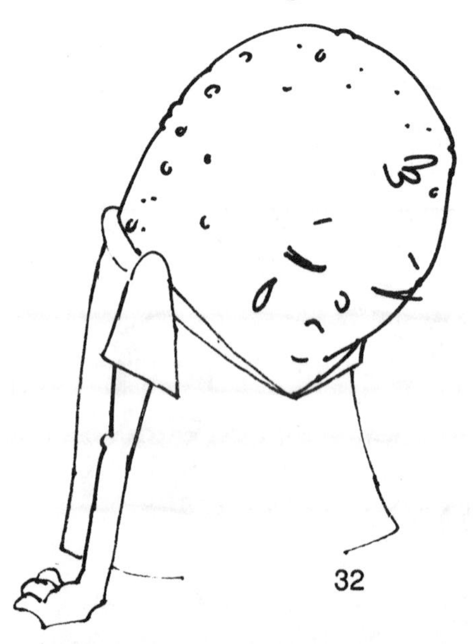

That night, after Hickle went to bed, she called her boss.

"I have a problem. I'm helping a friend do a research paper on where pickles come from. Do you know where I could get information to help? I've gone to the library and can't find out anything."

"Yes, there's a place in Illinois called Pickle Packers International, Inc. They will help you, I'm sure. I'll give you the address tomorrow at work." Sarah didn't tell Hickle about it. She didn't want to disappoint him any more.

The next day at work, the boss handed her a note with the address and phone number on it. After she picked up Hickle and got him outside to play, she called them.

"Hello. My name is Sarah Washburn and I would like some information on the origin of dill pickles. Do you have any information you could send me?"

"Yes, I'll be glad to send you what we have." Sarah was delighted. She wanted to tell Hickle, but preferred to keep it a secret until she received the information, and made sure it was what he needed.

A couple of days went by and Hickle was still sad. He walked around with his head hanging down. He didn't want to eat or play. Sarah went to the mail box every day. Finally, one day there was a large envelope from Pickle Packers International. She opened it and right there on the first line, it told about the origin. Sarah called to Hickle who came in running.

"What, Sarah? I'm building a castle," he said, out of breath.

"Come sit down with me. I have something for you." She showed him a book with jars of pickles on the cover and Hickle looked up at her, his big eyes shining.

"What's this?"

"Hickle, it's a book about your family. It tells where your family comes from and how far back. Hickle, you have a heritage.

You're famous! Now, go and wash your hands and I'll read all about your family to you."

Hickle went to the bathroom, washed his hands and climbed up on Sarah's lap as she opened the book and read him the story of pickles. Hickle felt tears trickle down his face as she told him that pickles go back to approximately 2030 B.C., and that they were brought to the Tigris Valley by the people of India.

"Where's the Tigris Valley?" he asked. Sarah went over to the globe and showed him. She also showed him where India was, and where Jimmy was born. Hickle never thought about coming from THAT FAR AWAY!!!

"How did we get here?" he asked.

"By boat, probably during the 17th century, it says here."

"My gosh, maybe I came over on the Mayflower with Columbus."

"Maybe," she said. As she continued to read, Hickle snuggled in her lap.

She showed him a picture of other relatives, Kosher dills, overnight dills, processed dills, sour pickles, whole sour pickles, sweet pickles, sweet fresh cucumber pickles, Polish-style dills. Hickle had no idea he had such a big family.

"Then there are relishes."

"What's that?"

"That's pickles chopped up with other vegetables."

"Ouch! That must hurt," he said with a twisted face.

"Oh, Hickle, they don't feel a thing. They aren't like you. They are grown just to be what they are, relishes and pickles." Hickle understood because he was supposed to be one of the specially-grown pickles. But all the love those little boys gave him in the back yard garden, plus the love Sarah gave him, turned him into a real little boy. He was happy that he didn't turn out to be just a pickle. He looked at the book about his heritage again and turned page after page. He also found out that from May 21st to May 31st is National Pickle Week. He was proud to have a family!

"Will you help me write a story about MY family? I think I'll take this book to school to show the kids where MY family came from." Sarah felt proud that she helped Hickle find his roots.

Two days before Thanksgiving vacation, the kids turned in their papers on their heritage. Hickle's won! It was the best story and he had the longest family history. He was selected to read his story to the children after recess the next day. Sarah asked if she could leave work early so she could be there.

The next day, Hickle stood in front of the class with his new dress pants and his bow tie. He looked so cute as he cleared his throat to read his paper.

"Boys and girls, I'm really a dill pickle. Due to some strange thing, I've turned into a little boy, just like you. I prayed I would be a little boy, and here I am. The reason I'm green is because pickles are green. My ancestry goes back to 2030 B.C., in the Tigris Valley." He went over to the map and showed them. "I belong to a large family and they live in different states. I also have some relatives which are sweet," he laughed. "We even have a special week, May 21st to May 31st,

National Pickle Week, where they honor pickles. I'm thankful for being here with all of you. I'm thankful to be alive and have a family and friends. I'm thankful that all of you are healthy and happy. Some of you have unhappy homes, but if you work hard, you can get past that, like I did. You can be anything you want to be if you try hard enough and work at it. I became a little boy from a pickle and nothing can be harder than that. Just have faith and it will happen. I'm very lucky! Thank you and have a Happy Thanksgiving."

The boys and girls all looked over at the boy who was always making fun of Hickle. He felt bad that he was such a bully and had hurt Hickle many times. He got up and went over to Hickle, held out his hand and said, "I'm sorry, Hickle, for all the things I did to you. Will you forgive me?"

Hickle looked at him. All the other boys and girls looked at him also.

"Yes, I'll forgive you. You and I can be friends."

The other boys and girls all joined hands and danced around Hickle singing, "Hickle's funny and we all love him. Hickle's funny and we all love him." Hickle stood proud with a big smile on his face, tears streaming down his cheeks.

On the way home, Hickle sat looking out the window. It had been quite a day. He looked up at the sky, watching white things float down on the car. He looked at the road, seeing the white stuff build up. Sarah proudly looked at Hickle. He had come a long way in the people world.

"What's the white stuff, Sarah?"

"It's snow, Hickle."

"It feels cold like a refrigerator out here." he said, getting out of the car.

"This is called winter, and there will be lots of this white, fluffy stuff before it warms up. Later, when we have more snow, I'll show you how to build a snowman."

"A snowman! What's that and can he play with me?"

"Who knows," she said, thinking, "Who thought a pickle could ever talk? Who's to say a snowman can't play? In this world, anything goes, and does."

The End

BEING COOL, GOING TO SCHOOL (rhyme)

by

Josephine A. Smith

The breeze felt good on Hickle's head
As he grabbed his blanket and snuggled in bed.
Thoughts circled around in his head
Of when he was born, lost and fed
His first ice cream cone of sheer delight,
The day he was found and brought home that night.
Of how he learned to live with the rule
Of responsibilities, work and school.

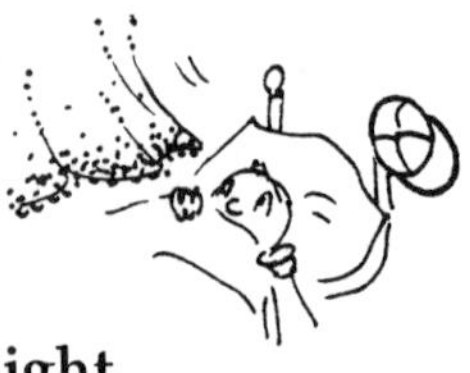

Now was the day he would go away
To a building big and tall
Where there was no one he knew, no one at all.

He was as scared as could be,
And wished he could stay home and watch TV.
But he knew he must learn to read and write.
He found THAT out that awful night
When he was lost and couldn't read that sign
Of where he lived on William Street, ten-o-o-nine.

"Time to get up," she said cheerfully,
As Hickle pulled up the blankets over his head,
And wished that she'd go back to bed.

Soon he was dressed and fed, ready to go
To a school building somewhere, he didn't know.
Away from Sarah, home and fun
And he hoped he would see her when day was done.

He looked back at his bed where he laid his hat and tie.
He couldn't wear them NOW, and he didn't know why.
Instead, he wore jeans, shoes and socks
And felt uncomfortable, all itchy and hot,
Unlike just a hat, shoes and a tie.
He felt scared with tears in his eye.
"I don't feel so good," he said as he started to cry.
"You've just got butterflies in your stomach," she said
As she locked the door, and patted his head.
"How'd they get in there?" he said,
Covering his mouth and feeling his head.
"I don't remember seeing them in my food.
Hey, maybe they just crawled in there to change my mood."
"Oh, Hickle, that's just an expression," she said
As Hickle sat in the car, wishing he was dead!!!

In the distance, he spotted his school
He remembered he'd have to follow their rule,
Learn everything he could and try to be cool.

But his worst fears were there inside.
Kids sitting around hurting his pride,
Calling him names because of his color
'Cause he was green, not white, black or yeller.

He had no friends to play with out on the bars
And he remembered the night he slept under the stars
With hope in his heart and love all around.
He was alone then, till he was found.

Then he felt a tap on his shoulder
There stood a boy, a little bit older.
"Want to be my friend?" he said in a quiet voice,
"I'm all alone too, and not by choice."

"I have no friends. They all laugh at me.
I've tried to be nice and to wait and see,
But they all laugh 'cause, I'm different, you see!"

"I don't think that's very nice at all.
They'd probably laugh, though you were thin and tall.
I guess it doesn't really matter what you look like,
I just wish I had lots of friends like MIKE!
He's so popular everyone likes him
He's not fat, tall or thin,
He's just right. I guess that's what's in!!"

"Well," said Hickle, "I'm just a little guy, but the wrong color."
"So am I," said Jimmy, "they all call me yeller!
Let's forget about them and have some fun
Let's swing and see if we can touch the sun!"

Everyday they played. They were the best of friends
From school's opening till school's end.

Later in the school year, the teacher drew a scene
It was a witch on a broom and a word HALLOWEEN!!
"Friday's Halloween," she said with a smile
"I'd like you to dress up for awhile."
"What's Halloween?" Hickle asked Mrs. Wicker
Amid laughter and a snicker.

"Hey, he must have come from Mars,"
Said one of the boys on the bars.

"Now boys and girls, quit poking fun,
Not all children know how Halloween is done."

"Hickle, for your homework, you will find what Halloween
Means. You can tell me alone, so there won't be a scene! "

That night Hickle and Sarah went to a library
Where he met a librarian named Larry.
The building was beautiful, big and bright
Where they stayed most of the night.
He never saw so many books before on one shelf
And wondered if he'd ever be able to read all by himself.

He found out all about Halloween
About a plowman that sounded real mean.
He was scared to go trick or treating
In case the plowman would come from a meeting.
"Hickle, there's nothing to fear," she said to herself
As Larry put the big book back on the shelf.

She left, feeling really good inside
But all Hickle wanted to do was run and hide.

He told the teacher what he had found the next day,
She was happy and gave him an A.
Then reminded him to dress up the next day.

Today was Halloween and Hickle wanted to stay,
He didn't want to dress up, no way, no way...
He didn't like to dress up and go to school
He was going to stay home, he was no fool.
If the plowman was out looking around,
Hickle wanted to make sure HE wasn't found!!

Sarah laid out a costume for him to wear
But Hickle wouldn't dress in that, he was going
NOWHERE!!

"What can I do so you will go
To school and the Halloween show???"

"I need something scary where I can hide,
Something that will cover me up, where I can be inside."

Sarah thought and thought.
Nothing fit that description that she had bought.

She looked at him hiding in bed,
Then an idea filled her head.
"How would you like to wear your sheet instead?"

"I can wear this to school?
Would I still be cool??"
"Yes, you can be a ghost, that's the most!
Now, you'll be safe, you can even wear your hat!!"
"Well," said Hickle, "how about that!!!"

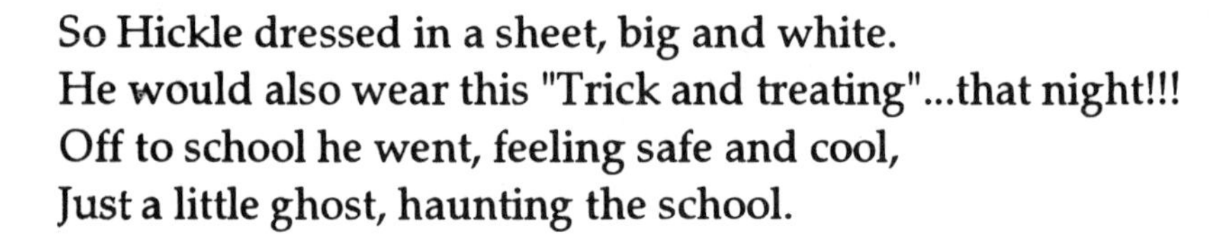

So Hickle dressed in a sheet, big and white.
He would also wear this "Trick and treating"...that night!!!
Off to school he went, feeling safe and cool,
Just a little ghost, haunting the school.

Later that night, Hickle had never seen so much candy.
And carrying that plastic pumpkin came in real handy.
Then he and Sarah sat on the floor sorting it all out.
Some he could have, some was thrown out.
Soon he was full and feeling kind of sick inside,
So he gave Sarah a kiss and went to bed with pride.
He was as full as he could be
From popcorn balls, gum and chocolate candy.

The next day the teacher had a project for the class.
"I would like you to find out about your ancestral past.
Soon it will be Thanksgiving
And I would like to know where your ancestors were living.
Some of them came from across the sea
Maybe from England, France or Italy.
We will make an ancestral tree
And put it on the wall for everyone to see."

Hickle raised his sad little hand
"My roots are in a garden. I came from the land..."
"Well," she laughed, "Maybe you can find out all about pickles.
I'm sure there must be a history about them, Hickle!!"

"Okay" he said, feeling really sad inside.
Again he wished he could just run and hide.

Where could he find out about pickles? Hey, he could ask Larry.
He would ask Sarah if he could go to the LIBRARY!!!

"Sarah...Sarah," He yelled as he ran for the car.
"Can we go someplace, someplace that's far?
I've got to go and find Larry.
I've got an important job at the library.
I've got to find out all about pickles,
To find my roots, because I'm a Hickle.
It's our project for Thanksgiving
To find out where our ancestors were living."
"Well," she said, as she sped down the street,
"We'll stop first and grab a bite to eat,
Then we'll go to the library, and see if we can
Find your friend, Larry."

Soon they entered his favorite building, big and white,
Looking for Larry, but he was off that night.
"Can you help me find the origin of pickles?"
Asked Sarah, as the librarian looked down at Hickle.
"Let's go to the book file,"
Where they stayed looking awhile.

"There are books on pickling, stories about pickles
But nothing on the origin," she said again, looking at Hickle.

"But I've got to find out about my ancestry.
You see it's real important to me.
It's also a school project for Thanksgiving.
We have to find out where our ancestors were living."

"I'm sorry that's all we have here,"
As Hickle turned around with a tear.

"I know we would have found it with Larry.
He's so smart he would have found it in that library!"

"Is there someplace else we can go
To find out about pickles, so I'll know?"

"Tomorrow I'll call the state library
And I'll ask them, it's called an inquiry."
She said looking at him, as he sat with a big grin.

The next day, when Hickle was away,
Sarah called but found no information
Or anything about Pickles...his relation.

She contacted a place called Pickle Packers International
Who said they would send information across the nation,
They would send her an answer right away
And she would receive it the very next day.

Next day, there was his answer as big as could be,
Pickles go all the way back to 2030 BC!!!

Next day, Hickle stood in front of the class as proud as could be,
All the kids gathered around him, 'cause he had the longest History.

Now he has friends some big, some small
But he loves them, he loves them all.

He loves everyone in school.
And everyone knows Hickle and thinks he's real cool!!!

Can you draw a picture of Hickle?

Can you write a story about Hickle?

Hickle is hiding in this pickle vine. Can you help find him?

**Jimmy is Hickle's best friend.
Can you color him?**

Now draw a picture of your best friend.